Super Ben

Written and illustrated
by Steve Smallman

Collins

Ben and his mum went to the park.

3

Ben drew a picture.

He fed the ducks.

He played on the roundabout.

He splashed in the puddles.

Then it was time to go home.

A story map

the park

No Swimming

the ducks

14

the roundabout

the puddles

15

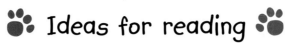

Ideas for reading

Written by Linda Pagett B.Ed (hons), M.Ed
Lecturer and Educational Consultant

Learning objectives: extend vocabulary, exploring the meaning and sounds of new words; retell narratives in correct sequence, drawing on the language patterns of stories; show an understanding of the elements of stories, such as main character, sequence of events; hear and say sounds in words in the order in which they occur

Curriculum links: Personal Social and Moral Development: Understand that there needs to be codes of behaviour

High frequency words: and, his, went, to, the, a, on, h, the, home, then, it, go, was, time, what, did, do

Interest words: puddles, park, roundabout

Resources: a whiteboard

Word count: 33

Getting started

- Look at the covers and discuss the picture. Is this a real boy? Discuss Superman, Spiderman or any other superheroes and what they can do.

- Point to the words in the title and read them together.

- Read the blurb on the back cover and ask the children if they've ever been to the park. What did they do? Who did they go with?

- Look at the pictures and encourage the children to point to Ben.

- Discuss the thought bubbles. What are they for? What is happening in them? Which is the real Ben and which is imaginary?

- Introduce words such as *shark, Martian, outer space, dinosaur*.

Reading and responding

- Return to the beginning of the book and demonstrate reading, pointing to each word in turn. Encourage the children to follow with their fingers as you read.

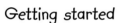